MW00929007

To "Team Jafu"

I couldn't have done it without you!

Britt, Tanya, Jenell, Vera, Karen, Judy, and Kim.

www.mascotbooks.com

A Giraffe in the Gym

©2016 Beatrice Brown. All Rights Reserved. No part of this publication may be reproduced, stored in a retrieval system or transmitted in any form by any means electronic, mechanical, or photocopying, recording or otherwise without the permission of the author.

For more information, please contact:
Mascot Books
560 Herndon Parkway #120
Herndon, VA 20170
info@mascotbooks.com

Library of Congress Control Number: 2016906370

CPSIA Code: PRT0616A
ISBN: 978-1-63177-634-2

Printed in the United States

A GIRAFFE IN THE GYM

Beatrice Brown

art by Alejandro Chamberlain

Something strange was bound to happen today.

It started when I hopped out of bed as soon as I heard Mom call me. No hiding under the covers, no "five more minutes, pleeeeease."

I was dressed and ready for school before breakfast was on the table.

The bus ride to school was uneventful, except for the fact that I was on the bus.

Mr. Wiley didn't leave me this morning. I was at the bus stop a full ten minutes before the bus arrived.

Yep, something strange was bound to happen today.

The school's internet was down, so Mrs. Davis asked Terrell and me to take the lunch report to the cafeteria and the attendance report to the office.

Terrell sighed. He knew I liked to stop and talk to other kids in the hall and take long, close looks at all the artwork that lined the walls.

highliter

We took the lunch report to the cafeteria and attendance report to the office. I didn't talk to a single kid the whole way and I only glanced at the art as we walked past it.

Five minutes later when we made it back to class, Terrell gave me a fist bump for moving so fast. Yep, things were going great.

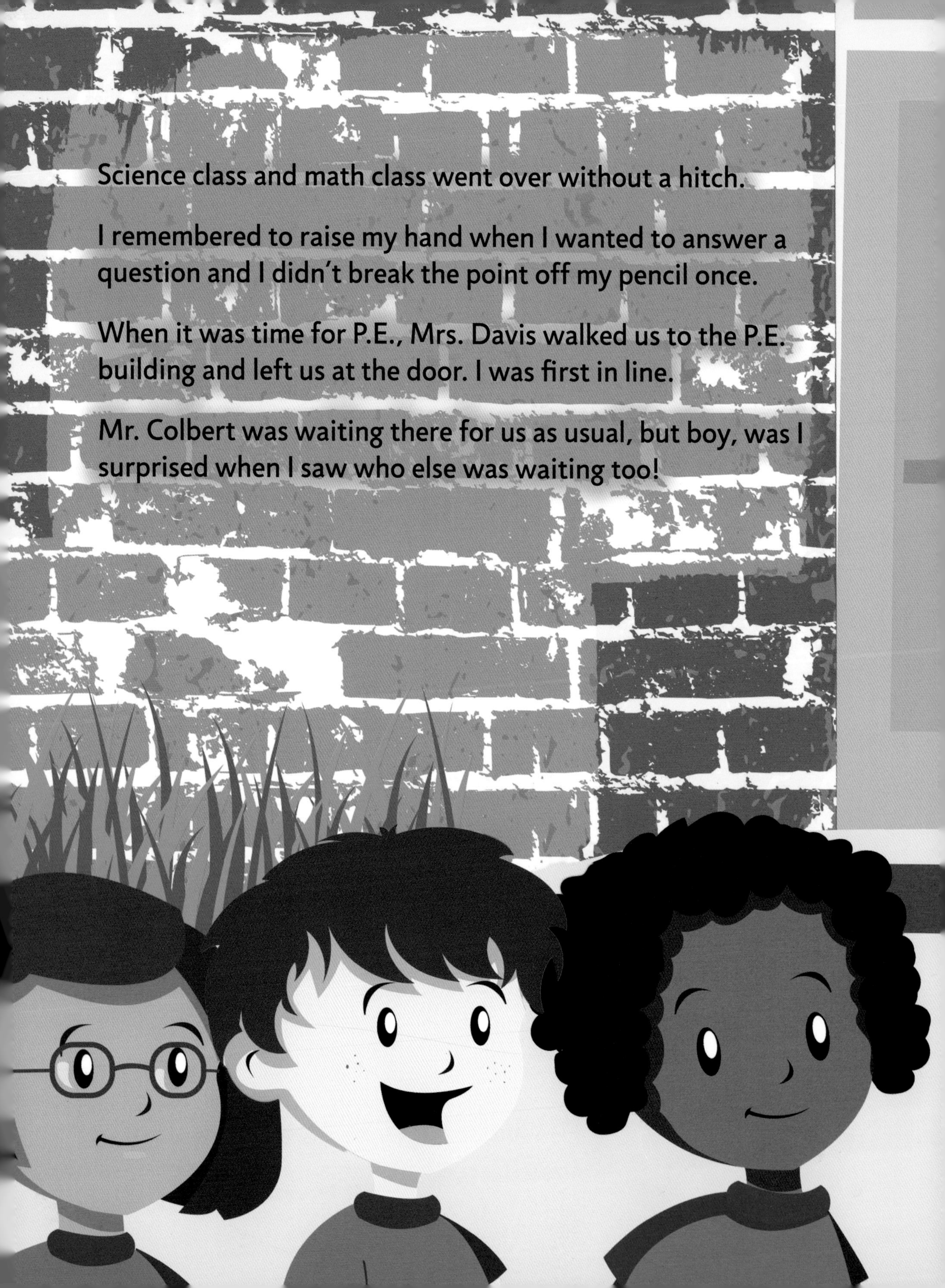

Science class and math class went over without a hitch.

I remembered to raise my hand when I wanted to answer a question and I didn't break the point off my pencil once.

When it was time for P.E., Mrs. Davis walked us to the P.E. building and left us at the door. I was first in line.

Mr. Colbert was waiting there for us as usual, but boy, was I surprised when I saw who else was waiting too!

Mr. Colbert held up his hand for silence before any of us could say a word. When Mr. Colbert asks for silence, he means SILENCE.

He went on with class as if it was perfectly normal for a giraffe to join us in our warm-up exercises.

Following Mr. Colbert's instructions, we did stretches.

"Arms up high...now touch your toes...arms out wide...now touch your nose.

Stretch...clap left...stretch, clap right...jump, jump, jump. Again.

Arms up high...now touch your toes...arms out wide... now touch your nose.

Stretch...clap left...stretch, clap right...jump, jump, jump."

We did the warm-up exercises five times until Mr. Colbert blew his whistle for us to stop.

"Breathe in. Breathe out. Breathe in. Breathe out," he said. "Again. Breathe in. Breathe out. Breathe in. Breathe out."

Mr. Colbert signaled for us to stop. He told Nick and Camille to pass out the jump ropes. We had been practicing jump rope skills for the past four weeks.

Everyone watched expectantly to see if the giraffe would take one.

Guess what? He did!

For starters, we did ***single jumps.***

From singles we moved to ***double unders.***

The giraffe was magnificent! Talk about an awesome jumper!

When Brittany suggested we jump ***Double Dutch***, we all held our breath.

The giraffe was first in line!

After everyone had a turn, Mr. Colbert blew his whistle and we moved to our assigned spaces against the wall.

"Let me introduce Jafu, the giraffe."

We burst into applause. Mr. Colbert and Jafu smiled, and after a minute of thunderous clapping, Mr. Colbert held up his hand for silence. Remember, when Mr. Colbert asks for silence, he means SILENCE.

"Jafu is here to introduce basketball, the next set of skills we'll work on in class," Mr. Colbert said. "Jafu will now demonstrate the five basic skills of basketball."

Jafu started with dribbling! He went in and out between all four of his legs! Then he stood at half-court and showed us how to shoot. Wow! He could dribble, he could shoot, and boy, could he run! Three steps and he went from one end of the court to the other!

Mr. Colbert joined him to show us how to pass the ball. Jafu demonstrated never-before seen moves!

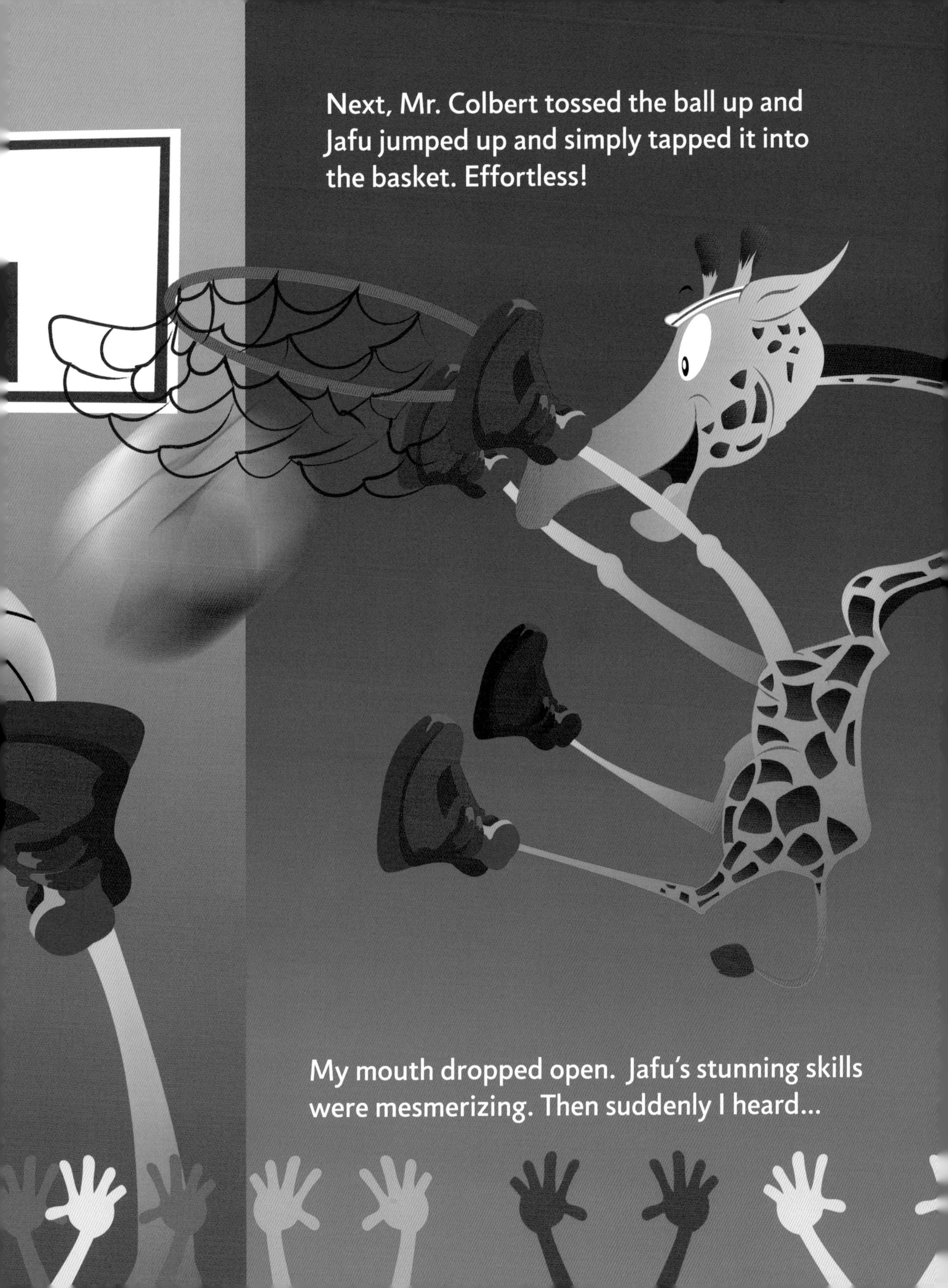

Next, Mr. Colbert tossed the ball up and Jafu jumped up and simply tapped it into the basket. Effortless!

My mouth dropped open. Jafu's stunning skills were mesmerizing. Then suddenly I heard...

What's she doing here? I thought as I looked around to see where she was.

"Brandon!" She was getting closer.

Then I felt her shaking my shoulder.

"You'd better wake up. You're going to miss your bus...AGAIN."

ABOUT THE AUTHOR

A retired educator with more than thirty years of experience in Special Education, Beatrice Brown has shared and laughed with children throughout the southeast. *A Giraffe in the Gym* and several other stories have been buried in her drawer while she served in her community and managed several projects for various organizations. She's excited to finally bring Jafu to life. She enjoys reading, writing, and traveling.

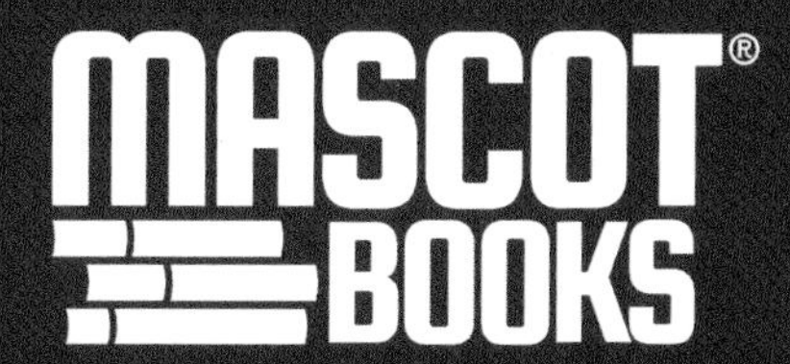

Have a book idea?
Contact us at:

Mascot Books
560 Herndon Parkway
Suite 120
Herndon, VA 20170

info@mascotbooks.com | www.mascotbooks.com